The Wizard Mouse

Library of Congress Cataloging-in-Publication Data
Morrissey, Dean.
    The wizard mouse / story and pictures by Dean Morrissey ; written by Dean Morrissey and Stephen Krensky. — 1st ed.
        p.   cm.
    Summary: A field mouse travels far from his home and helps restore a wizard's magic, thus saving the kingdom of Muddmoor.
    ISBN 978-0-06-008066-2 (trade bdg.) — ISBN 978-0-06-008067-9 (lib. bdg.)
    [1. Mice—Fiction.   2. Wizards—Fiction.   3. Magic—Fiction.]   I. Krensky, Stephen.   II. Title.
PZ7.K883Wiz   2011   2010012632
[Fic]—dc22   CIP
                                                                                                                                          AC

Typography by Jeanne L. Hogle
11 12 13 14 15   SCP   10 9 8 7 6 5 4 3 2 1
❖
First Edition

Dedicated to my dear friend
Carl Layman—a carpenter and a wizard

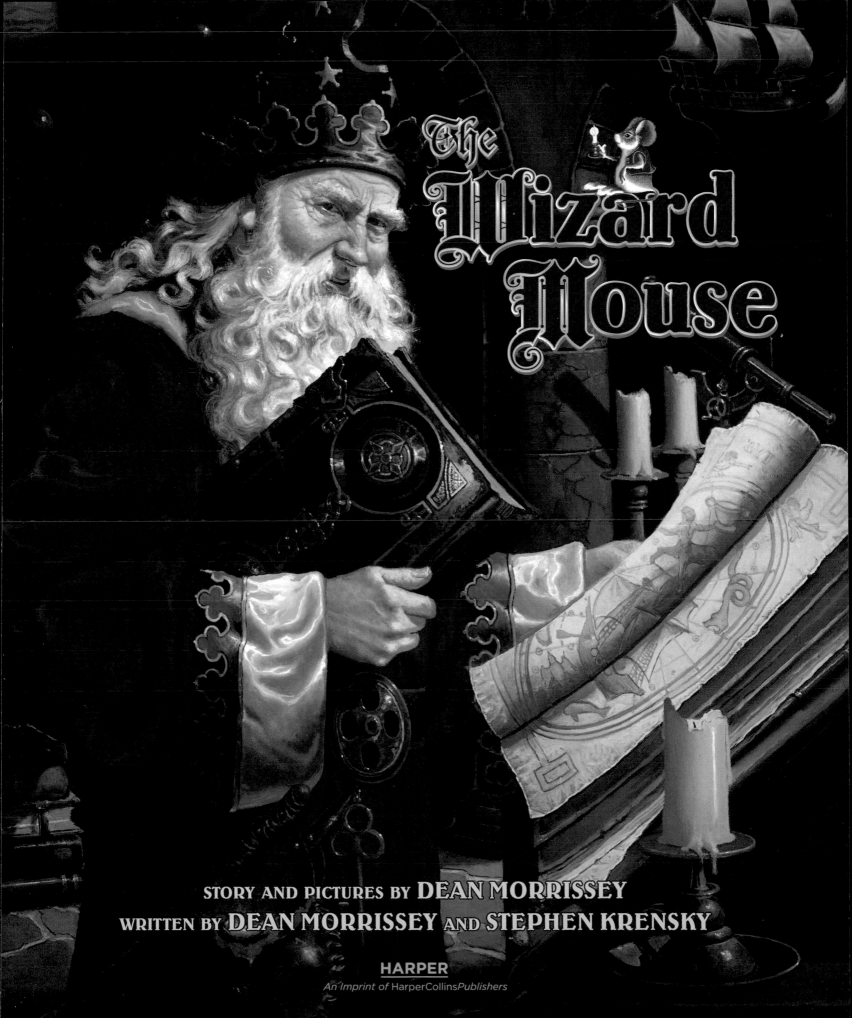

The Wizard Mouse

STORY AND PICTURES BY **DEAN MORRISSEY**
WRITTEN BY **DEAN MORRISSEY** AND **STEPHEN KRENSKY**

HARPER
An Imprint of HarperCollins Publishers

ollie looked around quickly and then began climbing the
fence post, making his way upward to the top. He could see the village of
Muddmoor, the castle, and past that the land that stretched out to the sea.
This dreamlike world called to him.

But, like his father and grandfather before him, Rollie was a field mouse.

"A mouse never need look beyond the field for his happiness," Rollie's
father would say.

But looking beyond the field was exactly what made Rollie happy.

"There's no corn to load up there," the field boss barked.

Rollie lost his balance and came crashing through the cornstalk, spilling his sack of corn kernels and landing at the boss's feet. Everyone laughed.

"That's it!" said Rollie. "I quit."

"Quit?" said the boss. "But you're a field mouse. This is your place."

"He thinks he's better than us," yelled a mouse.

Rollie said nothing and walked away from the only life he'd ever known.

Early the next morning, Rollie was off and walking down the long, crooked road that led to the Kingdom of Muddmoor.

Now, a mile to a mouse is a much longer walk than a mile is to a person. So, after walking a hundred yards, Rollie stopped to take a rest.

It was a long time until he came to open fields that gave way to forest. At the forest's edge, Rollie saw an apple tree, bent over under the weight of one gigantic apple. Rollie smiled. He knew he was a long way from the cornfield.

As darkness grew, he decided to stop for the night. He got under his blanket, ate some dried corn with a bit of cheese for supper, and fell asleep.

After a good night's sleep, Rollie rose and walked all the next day. Late in the afternoon he came to a beautiful tower, bending upward into the sky. A wooden sign hung above the door.

"WIZARD" was all it said. Two large cows were floating in the air above a clearing near the tower. What could this be? Rollie's curiosity was bubbling over. So he decided to slip in through the tower door to see what he could find out.

Huffing and puffing after climbing the long winding staircase to the top, Rollie spotted the wizard seated at a round table, reading a very large book. Just then, the wizard stopped reading and looked around as if he had heard something. Rollie froze.

The wizard walked right up to the peephole, closed one eye, and peered in with the other.

"Hello in there, my little friend," said the wizard. "Come on out where I can see you, now. Don't be shy. My name is Solarus."

Reluctantly, the mouse came out from the hole. "I'm, ah, Rollie the mouse. How did you know I was here?"

"Oh, don't feel bad, you were very quiet," replied the old man. "But after all, I am a wizard, and a good one, or at least I used to be." He shook his head. "Come into the library. I'm very glad to have a guest."

The mouse and the wizard talked
into the night. Rollie told of his journey
and life in the fields.

The wizard spoke of his two hundred or so years as the Wizard of Muddmoor.

He told the mouse of a recent battle of wits and magic with a Dark Magician for control
of the Kingdom of Muddmoor. Solarus had defeated the Dark Magician, but now he had no
magical abilities left.

"If word got out of my weakened state," explained the worried wizard, "Muddmoor could
be attacked.

"And, I must admit," the wizard continued,
"my memory for spells isn't quite what
it used to be, either. I've got hundreds of
them here in my books. Why, just today
I tried enchanting two cows who weren't
giving milk, and POOF, they vanished.
Haven't seen them since."

"Oh, I saw them," replied Rollie. "They were floating
above the field just outside."

"Yes, well," said the wizard. "You see what I mean."

"Perhaps I can help you," said Rollie. "In exchange for your kindness in letting me stay in your tower, maybe I could memorize your spells for you. Then, if you forget a spell, I could simply run up and whisper it in your ear."

The wizard laughed. "I suppose there's no harm in trying. Okay, mouse, you may help yourself to my spell books. I shall see you in the morning."

"Good night, sir," said Rollie. "You won't be sorry."

That night, Rollie read all the wizard's spell books and journals. He was yawning and about to stop when he picked up a leather book which told of ancient spells. One was of a magical fish. The book claimed that a person who ate the fish would be given great magical power and wisdom.

"That's it," said Rollie. "I'll catch the magic fish tomorrow, cook it for the wizard, and restore his powers."

In the morning, Rollie headed to a small pond outside the cottage with a pole in hand.

Soon a very large and splendid fish rose from the water. "You didn't really think you'd catch me with that hook and cheese trick, did you?" asked the fish.

"I was just trying to help my friend the wizard," Rollie blurted out nervously. "He lost his power and the book said if he ate you, he'd get it back and that could save the kingdom and . . . and . . ."

"All right, all right, calm down, mouse," replied the fish. "Those old books are very colorful, but your friend the wizard needs only to touch me to receive my magic. So let's get rid of the part where he eats me, okay?"

"Ah, sure," said Rollie.

"Very well, then," said the magic fish. "Take me to him. Muddmoor must be saved."

The mouse headed back to the wizard's cottage with the magic fish swimming happily through the air behind him.

"We're almost there," said Rollie. "Solarus is going to be surprised to see you."

Just then, a crashing sound up in the trees startled them both.

First a great golden star fell to earth and dug into the ground next to the pair. Then another. Finally a great metal dish, with the face of the moon, banged and cracked its way through the trees. Then all was quiet.

"We'd better hurry," said the mouse. "I'm afraid the wizard is trying to fix something."

When Rollie and the fish reached the cottage, they found the wizard scratching his head. A broken star sat in a vise on his workbench.

"Oh, what was that spell for enchanting stars?" he said in frustration.

"Wizard, I've brought someone for you to meet," Rollie began. "He's a magic fish and he's here to help us. Solarus the wizard, meet, um . . . the fish. . . ."

"Lear's the name. I'm the legendary Magic Salmon," the fish spoke up. "I've come to restore your magic."

"It's hard to explain, but if you would touch him on his back, like this," said the mouse, touching the fish, "you won't regret it."

"Oh, very well," said the wizard. Rollie watched him touch his long finger to the fish. Immediately a flush of electricity coursed through the old fellow. He seemed to glow from within.

"No one shall know that we met," said Lear.

The wizard wanted to thank the magic fish, but before he could, the magic fish . . . vanished.

The wizard's eyes were wide. He smiled and touched his face. "I haven't felt like this in years, mouse!" said the wizard, almost in a whisper. "Why, if I don't enchant something soon, I'm going to burst!"

He ran to his workshop, with Rollie at his heels, and raised his arms. "Constallatio!" he commanded the star.

Nothing.

The mouse ran up the wizard's robe and whispered the spell he'd memorized from the book.

"Yes, of course," replied the wizard. "ILLUMINOUS STRATOSPHERIOUS!"

Suddenly, stars and moons floated toward the window into the sky.

"My magic has been restored!" announced the wizard. Then he turned to Rollie with a smile. "Apparently not my memory, though, eh?

"Thank you, my little friend," said Solarus. "Because of you, the Wizard of Muddmoor has been restored. With a proper wizard, the Kingdom of Muddmoor is safe. The people and all the animals have you to thank, including those field mice who doubted you."

Rollie was speechless.

"You know, mouse, you touched the fish also, which means you now have the power of magic. That, along with your good, stout heart, makes you a very powerful little fellow. I hope you'll stay. You can learn from me and help me with such things as, well, my memory. I would be proud to appoint you to the position of Wizard Mouse. Top Mouse of the Kingdom! What do you say?"

Rollie took a deep breath. "Yes. Yes, I will."

And so it was decreed in the village square of
Muddmoor that Rollie the mouse was henceforth to be
known to all creatures of the kingdom as:

Rollie the Wizard Mouse,

Official Wizard Mouse of the Kingdom of Muddmoor,

In charge of all Wizardly dealings with mice of the kingdom,
including all field mice,

and Special Consultant to Solarus, the Wizard of Muddmoor.

"Well, my young Wizard Mouse," said Solarus. "With so many
things to do, where do you think we ought to begin?"

"Well," said Rollie, "we might want to do something about those floating cows."